To Preston Joshua Stokes,

May you always feel
safe and warm and loved.

Karen Goff Dyser   2011

To Preston Joshua Stokes,

To: _____

From: _____

Bailey Bunny
and the Fear Monster

A STORY OF COURAGE

By Karen Goff Dyser

Illustrated by Mary Ann Bucci

Halo
Publishing International
www.halopublishing.com

Library of Congress Control Number: 2010916886
ISBN 978-1-935268-81-9

Halo
Publishing International
www.halopublishing.com

Printed in the United States of America

To my children, Christopher and Cheryl,
my grandchildren, Morgan, Conner, Grant, Brandon, Laine, and Alex,
and to my husband, Joe, for his continued love and encouragement.

— KJD

To the joys of my life: my husband, my children, my grandchildren and the
little bunnies in my garden.

— MAB

Mama Bunny has a new Baby Bunny. She calls him Bailey. In their warm, cozy house, she rocks him in her old green rocker and sings, "Go to sleep my baby, close your little eyes. Mama's going to rock you and sing lullabies."

Bailey Bunny sleeps in his blue and white striped pajamas. He likes the rocking. He takes a deep breath and snuggles against his Mama.

He feels safe and warm and loved.

7

As Bailey Bunny grows, Mama rocks him and reads little books to him. He likes looking at the pictures and listening to the words. He likes the rocking and the reading.

He feels safe and warm and loved.

As Bailey Bunny grows bigger, Mama gives him a little red rocking chair that is just his size. Mama says, "Bailey Bunny, you are growing bigger and you can rock yourself now." He loves rocking in his very own chair.

He feels safe and warm and loved.

As Bailey Bunny grows bigger, Mama puts his basket of books beside his rocking chair. Mama says, "Bailey Bunny, you are growing bigger. Now you can rock yourself and look at your books." Bailey Bunny loves to rock and read his books.

He feels safe and warm and loved.

But, one night, after Bailey Bunny is tucked into bed, he suddenly awakens. Someone is taking away his little red rocking chair. Bailey Bunny cries, "Oh no, what can I do? A scary monster is taking away my rocking chair. I love to rock in my chair. I can't breathe. Mama, help!"

Mama rushes into Bailey Bunny's room. She holds his hand and then gives him a big hug. "There, there, Bailey Bunny. You are just having a bad dream. You're fine. Everything will be okay."

"See, your chair is right here in your room." Bailey Bunny takes a deep breath. He feels safe and warm and loved.

Every day after lunch, Bailey Bunny rocks in his chair and looks at his books.

But, a few nights later, Bailey Bunny again awakens crying, "Mama, the scary monster is here again. He is taking my chair!"

Mama rushes into his room. She holds his hand and then gives him a big hug. "There, there, Bailey Bunny. You're having a bad dream again. You are fine. Everything will be okay."

"This scary monster in your dream is not real. It is just a picture in your mind caused by your feeling of FEAR."

"Tonight we're going to learn how to get rid of the Fear Monster. The next time this happens, just say, Fear Monster, get out of my dream!"

Then Mama takes from her pocket, a smooth, flat stone with letters on it. The letters are C-O-U-R-A-G-E. "What do those letters spell, Mama?" asks Bailey Bunny. "It is the word COURAGE", answers Mama. "Courage means knowing, in your head and in your heart, that you have the power to stand up to scary things like the Fear Monster. You are strong, Bailey Bunny. You just have to believe you are."

Mama kisses the stone and says, "Keep this stone under your pillow. When that Fear Monster appears in your dream, hold this stone against your cheek and remember Mama's kiss. This will give you the courage to tell the Fear Monster to get out of your dream."

"Then wrap your arms around yourself, like this, and give yourself a big hug. You will be fine. Everything will be okay."

Bailey Bunny slips the stone under his pillow and takes a deep breath.

He feels safe and warm and loved.

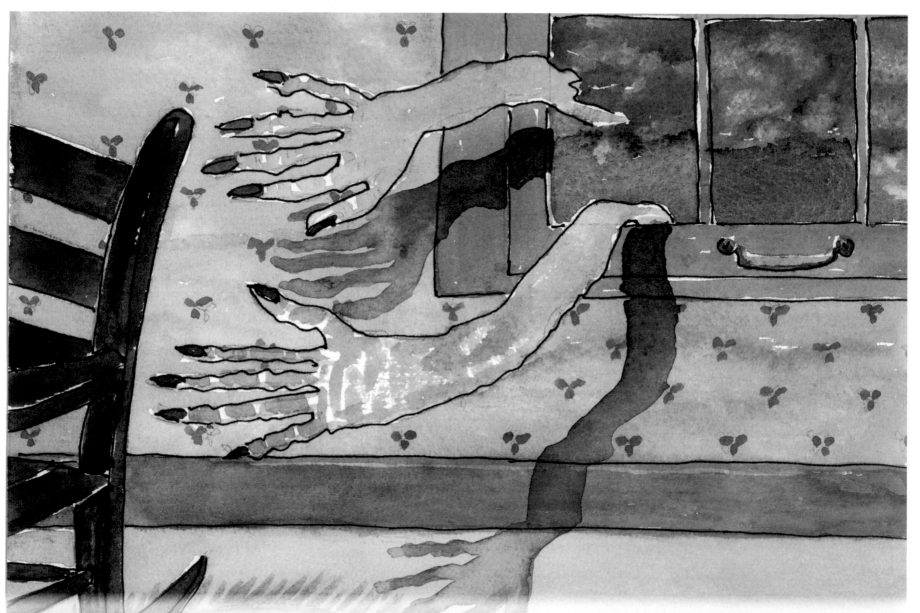

A few nights later, Bailey Bunny is sleeping. Oh no, the Fear Monster is reaching toward his chair!

But this time, Bailey Bunny reaches under his pillow, grasps his stone, and puts it up to his cheek. He remembers Mama's kiss AND he remembers that he has *courage*, in his head and in his heart.

Bailey Bunny yells, "Fear Monster, you cannot have my chair. Get out of my dream!" At once, the Fear Monster disappears.

Bailey Bunny gives himself a big hug and takes a deep breath. He knows that he is fine. Everything will be okay.

He feels safe and warm and loved.

Here are some questions for you to discuss with your parent, grandparent, teacher, or counselor.

1. What makes you feel afraid?

2. What do you do when you feel afraid?

3. How could you use a **courage** stone?

4. Can you draw a picture of the Fear Monster?

5. Can you draw a picture of the tree outside Bailey's window? Don't forget to draw the shadow.

6. What does that shadow look like? Look on page 26.